Cam always knows when there's a case to be solved!

"I have to show Dr. Prell something," Cam said. "It's about the loud noise."

Ms. Benson told Danny he could go. Then she whispered to Dr. Prell that Cam had something important to show her.

"Watch this," Cam told Dr. Prell. Then she pushed the large yellow book off the desk. It fell to the floor, but it didn't fall flat. First the edge of the book hit the floor. Then it landed on its side.

Dr. Prell was annoyed. She told Cam to pick up the book and get back to her seat. Cam picked up the book and said, "Didn't you see what happened? Books don't just fall. They must be pushed. And when they do fall, they don't fall flat and don't make a loud noise."

Dr. Prell looked at Cam. Then she looked at the book. She pushed it off the desk. It didn't fall flat.

"I think you're right," she told Cam. "Come with me. We'll talk to one of the Secret Service agents."